MW00898627

I Love You Just Because

Written by Catrice Dennis
Illustrations by Asiyah Davis
Rendering Artist Shakyena Sterling

Life Chronicles Publishing
ISBN-13:978-0998911427
ISBN-10:0998911429
Cover Design:
Life Chronicles Publishing
Life Chronicles Publishing Copyright © 2018
http://www.mylifechronicles.org

Dedication

This book is dedicated to my Divine inspiration, guidance, and love.
To my children and family, I Love You Just Because!

My mama says she loves me just because.
I say just because what mama?
Mama loves you just because…

The sun shines just as bright as you.

I love you just because the rain drops are wet like sweet honey dew.

My mama says she loves me just because the grass is green, and the sky is blue.

I love you just because your hair curls up like the branches of a tree, within each curl lies a special frequency that holds the key to unlocking earths great mysteries.

Mama says,
"I love you just because the trees stand tall and proud
just like how I feel when I look at you."

She loves me just because birds can fly and fish swim in the deep blue sea.

I love you just because the flowers bloom every May.

My mama says, "I love you just because you are made of stardust, oh how magical are you!"

I love you just because the sun sets way up in the sky for the whole world to see.

I love you just because your smile brings light to my life, like the multitude of stars that shine in the night.

I love you just because the thunder and lightning
bring out the beauty of the storm.

I love you just because your eyes remind me of the moon so bright and full.

My mama says she loves me just because the wind blows a cool breeze on a hot summer day.
She loves me like a tall cool glass of homemade lemonade.

I love you just because you reflect the earth and the
earth is a reflection of you.
I love you just because you remind me of all the good
that still exist within humanity.

I love you just because you continue to show me how love is limitless and filled with infinite possibilities.

Do you know what I tell mama?
Well, I look at my mama and say, "thank you for loving me and I love you just because!" My mama says, "just because what baby?" I love you just because you are the greatest mama there could ever be!

Made in the USA
Lexington, KY
21 March 2018